DIKE'S PLIGHT

DIKE'S PLIGHT

FRANK UZOMA AKWARA
The Author of CARAMEL

by

B

BOOKFIELD PUBLICATIONS. (NIG.)
www.bookfield.gnbo.com.ng

DEDICATION

To the memory of my late grandfather.
ANDREW N. AKWARA.
An Eternal Hero.

BOOKFIELD PUBLISHERS, (NIG.)
112, Adeshina Street,
Ijeshatedo-Surulere
Lagos.

TEL: 08028435914
E-MAIL: bookfieldconsults@yahoo.com
www.bookfield.gnbo.com.ng

Designed & Printed   By:
ROKAFOSH
Press Ltd

100, Adesina Street
Ijeshatedo Surulere, Lagos
TEL: 08033279587, 07083337646

Dike's Plight

ISBN: 978-978-927-940-1

CONTENTS   **Page**

Chapter One

Dike's Agonies

Dike Iwuala could not help the condition in which he was. This condition was as a result of his evil past. He felt superior to everyone and would do anything to destroy   the progress of others, especially those who thrived in their endeavors beyond his expectations. He engaged in a lot of bad and cunning deeds that had never happened in the great village of Aboh.

 In the eastern part of Nigeria, many villages and hamlets feared and respected Aboh people because it was rumored that they derived immense pleasure in eating human beings. Surely no intruder was in support of this practice.

Dike lived alone in a remote area in Aboh because everyone deserted him due to his wickedness. He loved it as it gave him all the privacy he needed to perpetrate his evil vices.

Dike looked highly depressed one morning after he had woken to find nothing for breakfast and had gone to bed the previous night with an empty stomach. He yawned in anger as the weakness caused by hunger almost made him fall, but the mud walls of his hut gave him support as he staggered out of the hut.

He shook his head and lamented, "chei! I am tired of this suffering," he said in self-pity.

"Imagine me in this village where everyone accuses me of being lazy. Do I really deserve all these? I swear by the gods I will fight anyone that says such stupid things about me again. Hopeless things!"

With weak bones, he dragged himself wearily back into his mud hut and sat down. He stared blankly, shrugged his shoulders and sighed, saying, "to show   selfishness, Uzonna a boy of yesterday cannot see my plight.   Dike iwuala, alias the clever 'mmbe' (tortoise) is in difficulty and will do something about it. Uzonna only thinks about himself and nothing else. He does not even care about the poor people in the village. Okay, I know what to do. The one and only mmbe will deal with him, 'Anofia' (foolish man)."

Dike could have sat there all day, but the sudden evil thought to harm Uzonna   propelled him to rise to his feet. He   was a clear example of an idle man that had become the devil's workshop.

He walked unsteadily as though the slightest breeze would blow him away and   hurried past the village market to avoid being seen, but unfortunately a group of little kids saw him and began to mock him by saying "mmbe go and work."   Usually, he would throw stones at them because this was not the first time the kids mocked him, but he was so weak that he could not give them a bad stare at least. He walked until he became tired of walking, but because he knew what he wanted and was so desperate to get it, he decided to crawl on his hands and knees.

As at then, those   who saw him crawling believed he had gone insane.

Dike moved until he got to the outskirts of the village, close to the entrance of an evil forest. In front of him some meters away, just as he had expected, was the shrine of Ezearu (king of evil) the evil and   notorious herbalist. He was also known as Ezemmo

(king of spirit).

Dike Iwuala met Ezearu in his shrine sitting on a sheepskin, crossing his legs and staring without blinking at the entrance as Dike crawled in.

"Good day, Ezearu" greeted Dike as he threw himself on the floor, exhausted from fatigue. "Greetings to you, what brings you here?" inquired Ezearu.

There was no way Dike could have started telling him why he came as a result of his helpless situation, but he managed to utter   "food, water.........please!"

Ezearu watched Dike, even if he was at the point of death, he could not have rescued him because he had to be released from his position by the spirits he served before he could do anything. This fault was from Dike   for not bringing anything to appease the spirits. Normally, all those who visited Ezearu for one reason or the other went with either kola nuts or palmwine to please the spirits. Ezearu had to plead on Dike's behalf before he was released minutes later.

Ezearu then attended to Dike and provided him with enough food and water to eat and drink before he could tell his reason for coming

"My son, you look like someone who has not eaten for days. What happened and why have you come to me?" Ezearu asked while Dike was still trying to regain enough strength.

Though Dike could not move himself very well as he needed enough time to be strong again, but he could talk loud enough for Ezearu to hear him.

"Ah! Yeeh! Thank you very much for your hospitality, I would have been dead by now" Dike said with relief. "Do you know that the last time I ate something was yesterday morning, and it was something a little bit bigger than a morsel of food. In fact I do not know how to thank you enough."
"But what stopped you from eating? Or is it that you don't have enough to eat at a harvesting season like this?" Ezearu questioned.

"That is why I've come to see you. I am almost at the point of death. There is a saying that 'the owl does not fly in the day time without a cause". I've been poor all my life because the villagers say that I'm lazy and nobody is willing to help. Instead, they go about gossiping with my name, me, Dike Iwuala, the one and only mmbe of Aboh," Dike said in anger as he beat his chest seriously.

He continued; "actually, my annoyance is on my late mother's ne-phew, a small boy whom I saw his date of birth" Dike boasted.
And what about him?" Ezearu asked.

He's too proud because he is prosperous, and instead of recognizing my condition and aiding me, he does not care a bit about me. So, now, I want him to know that no matter how rich he is, he is suppose to recognize his elderly relatives. I don't want him dead, but I want you to reduce him to nobody and let him taste hard ship."

Ezearu smiled as that was what he was known for, causing harm and killing with all pleasure. That's why he had the names Ezemmo (king of spirit) and Ezearu (king of evil). Before commencing his job, Ezearu had to consult the spirits of the dead, the living unseen's he served. He picked up some knotted

beads and began to wriggle them; he dropped the beads, clapped his hands and maintained silence. He repeated the act six times, showing that he had six spirits which he served. When he finally finished, he was happy but pretended that it was going to be tough, even after consents were granted to him by the six living invisibles.

"Look it will be hard to do something like this because the man you seek has done nothing against you", lied Ezearu.

"Please Ezemmo", pleaded Dike, "….do it for me, I'll do my best to meet up with your demands". Though Dike was too proud to beg anyone, but he had to plead with Ezemmo who was delighted to see someone beg him for a need.

Noticing Dike's desperation, Ezearu gave him conditions as to what he should pay to get the job done.

"Okay, these are the things you must do; you have to get some of his hair and some quantity of his urine, and lastly ......er..... you know I must eat too and get something for the spirits I serve, so your price is fifteen shillings," Ezearu told Dike plainly.

Dike was mute for a while because of the heavy price and task, but to harm Uzonna was what he really wanted in his life as a wicked and lazy man. Ezearu has read his mind and was very sure that he would never be able to pay the amount he requested, but he gave an alternative. He told Dike to work in his farm for twenty five days but should ensure that he got the other items for the rituals.

Dike seemed quite pleased as he was told to

pay with labour, and must do that if he really wanted Uzonna down.

The deal between Ezearu and Dike was sealed and Dike promised to start the work as soon as he got the required ritual items. On his way home through a narrow bush path, he was deep in thought and talked to himself, "I never knew it was going to be as tough as this. How do I get uzonna's hair and urine? As if that is not enough I have to work for twenty five farming days to ensure the payment of this thing. How am I to do these things? 'Nna' may be I should forget Ezearu and look for some other means. I believe in myself, the stubborn Mmbe. I know there could be some cheaper means to get what I want."

Dike did not want to return to Ezearu but Ezearu was a bad wizard-doctor who could never be turned down. He had powers to make someone long dearly for his assistance at all cost, so Dike did not stand the chance of escaping him.

Now, the Ndi-Nze (council of chiefs) of the village of Aboh reshuffled their chieftains annually. This was known as 'Oriri mmechi afor '(end of year ceremony), and it took place at the end of each year to thank the gods for seeing them through the year. During the ceremony, pledges were made for the coming year and new chiefs were usually coronated.   The annual routine happened to favour Uzonna as he was going to be made a chief that year, and when Dike found out, he was filled with envy. He cursed the name of Uzonna and started plotting even harder to bring him down.

He started spying on Uzonna every morning through a tiny and unnoticeable hole he made in Uzonna's bamboo fence. He would wake up as early as possible and run   to the place where he made the hole. Even as he hardly ate once a day, he did not mind because he was getting used to it. He endured   for over nine days until he got lucky one morning.

Uzonna woke very late and hastened to finish up his morning chores before leaving for the market place as it was a market day. In his hurry, he left his wooden comb outside in his compound and even forgot to lock his door after leaving. He wasn't anticipating anything unusual. Dike saw this and jumped at it. He quickly climbed over the fence and picking up the comb, extricated the strands of loose hair. He checked Uzonna's main hut to know if he could find something to eat but he did not, so he left cleverly without anyone noticing him.

He kept spying on Uzonna   without any one seeing him. Even if they did they may not think or believe that he was up to something as he was considered a nobody. The third day, after he had gotten the strands of hair, he obtained the second item Uzonna's urine. This was easier for Dike because he took note of chief Uzonna's bathing place. There was a small hole through which the waste water passed anytime he had his bath or urinated. All Dike did as a clever "tortoise" was to put a gourd at the end of the waste water passage, timing the moment that chief Uzonna would urinate. Sure enough Dike's urine trap caught its   prey. He wasted no time in taking the   items   to the impatient Ezearu after which he commenced work on Ezearu's farm as agreed.

Dike had problems with Ezearu after a few hours of working in the wizard's farm.

He could not cope with the stress of farm work and when he disclosed it to Ezearu, whose thought could not be determined from his evil looks, he told Dike to leave. He said he'd not be performing the rituals again and would not   hand over Chief Uzonna's urine and strands of hair. A dispute arose, threatening to shatter the scaled deal between the Mmbe and the wizard, but they settled their differences   and Dike was re-employed in Ezearu's farm land.

Both in agony and bitterness, Mmbe cursed as he worked reluctantly. He got injured many times as a result of not knowing the basic techniques of working with a hoe. It took him eighty five days to finally complete the work and   was lucky that Ezearu took care of his feeding through out his time of bitter experience; he may have died of starvation. This position has forced him to hate very single person he met. If he had his way, every Aboh villager would be dead especially Uzonna. His mind had been poisoned by people's behavior towards him and that made him   heartless.

Ezearu prepared the deadly spiritual weapon. It comprised of gazelle's horn filled with a mixture made with Uzonna's urine and hair strands.

It was then covered with a hawk's feather. The feather represented something that flew, so its function was to make the effect of the charm fly to
whom it had been prepared for. Before Ezearu handed it to Dike, he warned
Dike, "take it to the center of the 'achi' forest and buried it there. Call the
name of your enemy and
whish him anything you like for him. You can find the center of the 'achi'
forest near the big 'orji' tree, but if anyone gets to know about this you will
wander aimlessly until you're forgotten, I have warned you." "That is no
problem, I'll be very careful and no one will see it, thank you very much,"
Dike said with a broad smile on his face, the smile was only a camouflage;
in his mind he cursed Ezearu for charging him so much. Dike stood up and
left the shrine, vowing never to return there again.

Chapter Two

The Robbery

Uzonna continued to be more prosperous than he could imagine.

His trade was flourishing and his wealth increased in tens of folds. All
these added to his newly acquired chieftaincy title as the "ISHI AGU I" (LION
HEAD) of Aboh, the youngest unmarried chief there was amongst the entire
eastern region. He really deserved such honour because his good will fetch
him popularity, even as far as many distant villages. That was why despite
his age, he was made a chief.

On a cool night Chief Uzonna laid still as he slept in the best hut of his
forty-five-meter compound, snoring noisily in the late hours of the night.
Everywhere was so dark and quiet that one could here the crickets chirping.
The moon was absent so no kid stayed outside to play. A peaceful and quiet
wind was blowing to give every one a good sleep. Suddenly from the open
entrance of Chief Uzonna's compound, someone appeared. The intruder
took a careful peep after being sure that the place was clear, he nodded and
signaled two other people to join him.

The three of them tip-toed quietly to the smaller huts with the first man
holding a flaming oil lamp that provided them with light. They wore nothing
on their feet so that they would not make any sound and covered their
bodies with dark linen to match themselves with the dark night. After silently
breaking

into the first hut they were disappointed to see only working tools, the second hut had yams and the   other food stuff in it. They did not take any because their mission was to lay hands on anything portable and expensive.

By the time they got to the fourth hut, a hut which Uzonna had prepared for his awaited bride, they found expensive cloths and beads, bangles and silver treasures that were worth a fortune. Inside the hut also were Uzonna's titled beads and silver staff. The three desperate thieves took all the valuables and greedily went to check the largest hut, but there they found only six different species of livestock.

They did not want to go to the best and well designed hut as they knew that Uzonna would be there. Instead of wasting more time as they discovered that there could be nothing else to steal, they fled. They went away with all they stole to the forest at the outskirts of Aboh village where they camped.

Hours later, it was sunrise and   the Chief woke up after the   second cock crow, and his four hefty and hardworking servants had already come to work for him.

They did not seem to notice what had happened because all the items in the huts seemed intact and untouched. They began their day's work by feeding the livestock and getting ready the food stuffs that would be sold during the next market day-two days ahead.

The chief walked out of his hut with a thick brown and flowered wrapper covering his waist

downwards, and wore on his feet a pair of slippers made and designed with hyena skin. As he moved around in his compound with his left hand covering his mouth while he yawned, his servants saw   him and went on their knees and greeted him collectively. That was to show respect for an elder and a chief, as it was the tradition.   Uzonna acknowledged their greetings before proceeding. He walked around his compound and   into all other huts as if he had a strange feeling that something was wrong somewhere. On sighting the hut which was directly opposite his best hut, he   noticed that it had been tampered with.   The door was left ajar. In an aggressive mood he quickly rushed to the hut and discovered that the valuables in it were gone, they've been stolen.

"Dokaefe! Dokaefe!" he shouted, calling his Chief servant. "Nnanyi", he answered as he quickly ran to chief Uzonna and knelt in front of him.

"Who broke this hut and took everything in it" chief Uzonna hollered.

"Nnanyi, I am ignorant of who did it," the servant replied innocently.

"What! Shut up, go and call the rest," chief Uzonna roared in anger.

The servant did as he was ordered and came back a few seconds later with others. "Who broke this hut and took the things in it?" he asked repeatedly, but the servants all denied knowing anything about the theft.

"No it can't be, you   are the only ones that come into my compound very regularly, you're all thieves and I'm charging you for stealing to the village

council," Uzonna threatened.

All the servants began to cry, pleading with the chief as they knew the implications once they got convicted for theft. The sentence was death because it was forbidden to rob a chief. Chief Uzonna wasted no time as he got dressed and ordered his servants to follow him to the village council.

Mean while, in the forest where the thieves spent the night after making away with the things they stole, they were busy trying to sort out how to share the loot because they did not trust each other. Chinonso, the bravest and the leader suggested that they should sell the stolen goods and share the money, but the other two did not find it a good idea. They insisted that they shared the loot because they had different needs for each of the stolen items.

Chinonso agreed because he believed he could still sell his share and make use of the money. Everything was shared equally into three, except for a left over which was Chief Uzonna's silver staff.

There was no way   they would have split it except by cutting it which would render it useless. So at that stage, Chinonso decided that he'll keep it, since he was the leader.   Uche and Chidi, the other two disagreed, vowing that such   would never happen because he had been having the "lion's" share each time they finished stealing.

Chinonso insisted that he would have the staff whether they liked it or not, he packed his own share, grabbed the staff and stood up to go. The other two had always been afraid of him but as at then, they could not

resist ganging up against him. Initially, he tried to scare them as he used to by   making an aggressive move on Chidi, the weakest, but things changed. They were no longer   afraid of him and this he noticed when Uche advanced with a big stick towards him.

Chidi fetched his own too and Chinonso drew back, knowing that his leadership was over but he was not willing to let go of the silver staff. In a continuous pull back while calculating his steps, he quickly ran away with every thing he had. Uche and Chidi went after him to stop him from escaping with the staff. Chinonso ran as fast as he could but not too far from Uche who was seriously gaining ground on him, he was rapidly closing the gap as Chidi followed up closely. Uche stretched out his hand to reach Chinonso from a few meters while Chidi still followed closely. All of a sudden, the three of them felt themselves going down and seconds later, slamming against a lower level of the earth. Chinonso suffered it mostly because he was the first to hit the ground while the other two fell on him. The weight of the other two over powered him and he sustained a broken shoulder.

After Uche was sure of retrieving the silver staff form Chinonso, he realized that they had fallen into a pit, a deep one for that matter. There was no time for brawls anymore as they soon started thinking of how they would get out of the pit.

At the village of Aboh, Chief Uzonna had charged his servants to the village council for stealing. The council figured to carry out investigations through the village herbalists, since there was no eye witness

to the reported theft. The servants were kept under custody until the truth was discovered.

The herbalists started tracing the thieves from Chief Uzonna's house with their charms. They moved until they got to the forest because only the herbalists could see the thieves tracks. They found out the place were the thieves had camped and Chief Uzonna saw a few of his valuables which were the shares of both Uche and Chidi. They had left the items   to run after Chinonso.

"Where could they be?" asked Chief Uzonna

"I have a feeling that they could be around somewhere here because I still see their footprints," answered one of the herbalists. They then con-sulted their oracles as they moved on until they got to the pit where the thieves had fallen into. They were instantly convicted because the evidences that proved them guilty were right in their possession. The robbers were brought out, tied hands and feet and taken to the council hall, back in Aboh.

Chapter Three

The Cult

Chief Uzonna realized how wrong he was for the theft charge made against his servants. He became aware of his servants honesty and loyalty to him. He expressed his apologies to them, gave them back their job and compensated them with an increment in their wages for the shame he brought to them.

That night, after sunset, he made for an early night sleep when the town crier came with an important announcement "listen carefully all 'Ndi Aboh' (people of Aboh), the head chief, by the will of the gods, has told everybody to stay in his or her house by midnight. 'Oge ahu' (that time), the other chiefs are expected to gather for an important Nzuko (meeting). Anybody caught outside his compound will be punished without question." The town crier announced in his typical Ibo accent and continued after beating his gong.

The announcement went round the village and even to the notice of the lazy Mmbe, Dike. His reaction was; "the head chief must be joking. Imagine the time it took me to find the 'Oji' tree in the center of the forest and tonight is the night I've planned to carry out my mission. Only an earthquake can stop me tonight, after all, I am too clever for this village" Dike thought.

Chief Uzonna set out for the meeting as soon as it was midnight. The whole village looked empty as he walked along the way with the aid of the moonlight.

On reaching the council hall, a place that was also the palace of the headchief, he met all the other chiefs waiting for his arrival.

He was very surprised to discover that he was the last to arrive, despite reaching the hall some few minutes before midnight. Chief Uzonna greeted all of them but none gave a response, the reason was that their eyes were closed and they all maintained a still position like molded statues. Chief Uzonna was baffled because of what he saw. That was the first time he was seeing something like that, ever since he was made a chief. But he was yet to understand as he sat down and waited to see what would happen next.

At exactly midnight, the headchief came out from a small dark room in the palace and released the chiefs from their still position.

"Welcome, honorable chiefs of Aboh, I greet you all", said the head chief, but the other chief did not talk because that kind of meeting wasn't the kind that other chief could talk or do their will. The headchief did the talking and other things while the rest only listened attentively and obeyed orders. "As you all know, we've come here for a purpose, to conclude the welcoming of chief Uzonna Udo, the ISHI AGU I' of Aboh. Do feel free to shake hands with him in the presence of our ancestors," the headchief urged them. The chiefs went orderly to chief Uzonna and did the traditional greetings. They hit their staffs with Uzonna's thrice each, and followed it with hands shake. The headchief told them to take off their clothes and they complied remaining only the inner shorts they wore.

Chief Uzonna did the same, but did not

understand why. The headchief walked into the dark room, followed by the other chiefs, and of course chief Uzonna. Inside the dark room stood a seven- feet tall stone shrine and other mystical things hanging on the walls of the room. Their only aid to light was a little oil lamp.

"On your knees" ordered the headchief and they quickly obeyed and watched. The headchief closed his eyes and raised his hands before reciting some strange incantations. "With the strength from above and the strength underneath, I put them together to command the shrine to split" gently with a thin sound, the shrine opened. The recitation of the incantations was the only way to open the shrine and gain access into it. As foretold by IKE-CHIALA, the founder and herbalist that laid the shrine, the days in the shrine were faster than the days of the real world.

Ikechiala said the shrine was a way one could meet with the gods of the land and only the headchiefs could enter it. Many who lived and died in the village had heard about the shrine but they had not set their eyes on it, not even for once. It was said that the shrine could only be destroyed by those born on any day of anniversary of the shrine. So the villagers saw it a taboo for a child to be born on any of the shrine's day of anniversary, and any child born on any of the days was killed.

Now, the headchief entered into the shrine and a voice thundered within the shrine; "what brings you here my faithful one?" it was the voice of the gods of the land.

"Oh great one" said the headchief as he bowed.

"It is I, the headchief of Aboh land. I've come to submit to your excellent judgement, the thieves from Umudai whom we caught disturbing the peace of your children."

"Very well, my faithful one, do to them as you've been doing to others," the same voice thundered and echoed back, "great one, your whish is my command," said the headchief as he bowed and left.

When the headchief got out of the shrine, he told some of the chiefs to get the thieves tied up. They did so and the headchief sliced each of the thieves' throats with a sharp dagger. The other chiefs that already knew the activities and process, got a large gourd and collected the blood flowing from the corpses of the dead thieves

They all took turns each by sipping on the blood they collected. Chief Uzonna had been having a very difficult time after seeing what the other chiefs did, he had also heard about the shrine and rumors that his fellow villagers ate humans and drank their blood. What he saw was more than he could take, and when it got to his turn to sip from the gourd, he fainted. The other chiefs including the headchief were very surprised because nothing of such had ever happened, especially in the dark room during any of the shady meetings. The headchief called his name but he did not answer. He then recited some other incantations whilst placing his blood-covered hand on the unconscious Uzonna's head. Uzonna opened his eyes and sat up, but he was mute.

"Are you all right?" the headchief asked Uzonna. He had to show concern for him that moment

because the meeting was called especially to initiate him and to fulfill the promise they made to the gods by sacrificing the three thieves.

"I am alright," chief Uzonna spoke as he coughed. A meeting like that was a new thing to Uzonna, no wonder he behaved like a child who had seen a lion. No one hinted him on what to expect.

The headchief tried to build up his courage. "Look Uzonna, you're not hard hearted. Why don't you try to harden your heart? Strengthen the inner most part of you and be a strong man as your father used to be in his days. We all were once like you- afraid of what was going to happen if we partook on what was going on here, but today we are used to it and our forefathers are proud of us. Get a grip of your heart and act like a man because your failure to cope, especially in a short while, could take your life."

Chief Uzonna became aware that the rumors carried around by other villages and communities in the eastern region about Aboh were true. After discovering this fact, there was no way out for him. It was unfortunate that he had to unwillingly be a partaker, or else the penalty would be his death.

That same night, in the Achi forest while the meeting was going on in the dark room, Dike Iwuala successfully sneaked into the forest without anyone seeing him , it took him quite sometime to get to the center of the forest, and when he did he buried the charm and began his gruesome wishes for Uzonna. "I wish Uzonna to become careless about whatever that is important to him. I wish he fails and becomes poor, , and if all these won't be enough to destroy him totally,

he should die." He did everything according to Ezenmo's instructions and sneaked back home. Dike was really smart, just as a tortoise, slow and dangerous that even all the night guards that were on duty that night could not spot him.

Now in the dark room where Uzonna had been with the other chiefs and headchief, he, without further hesitation agreed to do whatever he was told to do. That was because the charm that Dike laid for him had already started to have its effects on him. Whatever he was told to do, he did it like someone hipnotized. He hadn't the power to control his actions again, even if in his mind there was little resistance.

Then the headchief took the dead thieves into the shrine one after the other. Coming out after a short while, the corpses became roasted and all the chiefs ate them with the headchief taken the lead, even chief Uzonna wasn't left out until the gourd was empty of blood and the chiefs having their fill.

The head chief went back into the shrine, .thanked the gods and made another statement that closed the shrine. "With the strength above and underneath I put them together and I command this shrine to unsplit." They had completed their practice for that day and the gods were happy with them.

The meeting ended with smiles on their faces, the chiefs came out and wore back their clothes. They shook hands and congratulated their new member, Uzonna, before dispersing to their various homes.

Chief Uzonna cared less about his worries and hardly remembered the things that were

important to him, including his business. Though in the cult of the chiefs, all members were made rich or richer by the ancestors as long as they continued the practice of the cult. Businesses or any source of live hood progressed for all the members, but, chief Uzonna's case became different, and this was due to the charm that Dike Iwuala made to ruin him.

Somedays later, while chief Uzonna was in his compound sitting and drinking palmwine, he heard the town crier's voice.

"Ndi Aboh, (people of Aboh) the headchief has called for an important 'Nzuko' (meeting) at the council hall for the chiefs. Starting immediately after sunset, everybody is free to go about but not near the hall."   Chief Uzonna only smiled after hearing the announcement, but showed a positive attitude and made up his mind to attend the meeting. He went for the meeting before the scheduled time and found that no one has come except him. He waited until some of the other chiefs arrived, walking pompously as if they were the gods themselves with their silver staffs. As matured men and leaders, they waited but not for long before the headchief came and commenced the meeting.

"Fellow chiefs and members of the living gods occults I greet you all," the head chief began.

"Greetings to you, Nzeukwu (headchief), and the gods," they all replied unanimously.

"Yes, long live the gods and peace shall reign, I think by now you ought to know that the gods are waiting for the payment of his promises you owe him and this is the time to pay back what you owe." The other chiefs did not seem to understand what the headchief was insinuating. A chief who had been confused like the others got on his feet and asked the headchief for some more explanation. The headchief smiled because he knew they would not understand in the first instance, but he began to explain more of what he meant to their understanding.

"Yes, I very much like your question and that will grant me the pleasure of answering you well so that you can comprehend. You've all been made chiefs, attained titles, honorable post and wealth, including prosperity, lest I forget. But you never for once thought about pleasing the gods for all these things and how you'd go about it"

"But Nzeukwu, you never told us anything about paying back for anything before we joined the cult," another chief protested.

"I wasn't supposed to tell you, because if I did, most of you would not have honored the chieftancy and the gods would not be happy. That's why I told you the advantages and left your payment for later", the headchief narrated more.

"Then how or in what way are we going to pay back to the gods?" asked the same chief who looked worried.

"That you'll soon find out" concluded the headchief." The headchief gave chief Obidike, his next in command the go-ahead to show the other chiefs how they'd pay back.

Chief Obidike went into the dark room and returned with a hen, a cock and a basket full of dried maize cobs.

"These things were given to me by the gods of the land through the Nzeukwu, all of you must come out and take a maize cob and then you will allow the hen and cock to feed on your cobs one after the other. When they take their fill on each of your cobs, the number of maize grains left on the cobs will be the number of years left for you to live before the gods would come and take your souls" chief obidike disclosed.

"Mmba (no), you can't mean that." Some of the chiefs protested.

"How can we do such a thing? Don't you know that we all have wives and kids to take care of, even relatives? If we die now they'll suffer," they said. "That does not concern me. After all I have wives and kids too. But if you decide to go against the tradition of your forefathers, you'll only have yourselves to blame. It would be better for you to take this chance now and have more days on this earth, than refusing and allowing the gods to come for you right now. You should reasonable, at least to know that the gods are being fair. In other words, whoever refuses to carry out this practice will die," the headchief concluded menacingly. There was no other alternative for the other chiefs, no where to run to and no place to hide. They had to comply even if it was reluctantly. Only chief Uzonna was less concerned about what would be the outcome of such a suicidal venture. That was because the charm was still working on him. Immediately the whole thing was over, chief Uzonna became the most fortunate man. He had ten corn

seed left on his cob while the rest had far below what he had. Even the chief whose number of corn seeds came next to chief Uzonna's own had five.

This had been a long practice amongst the chief and the cult. Even the present headchief went through the same process when he had not been made a headchief, and he had eight corn seeds left on his cob which means eight years. He had lived five years out of it.

CHAPTER FOUR

Uzonna Takes A Bride

Days passed after the regrettable meeting of the chiefs. After finding out facts about what chieftancy was all about, the chiefs discovered that being a chief was not something to be really proud of. It was then they knew why many chiefs died without definite causes, and surely, they too may end up dying without the villagers knowing what really caused their deaths.

Chief Uzonna, after his change of attitude, left people wondering why and how he changed. No one knew or suspected that he was being con-trolled by a charm; otherwise he could have been rescued. He cut a lot of his dealings with many of those he traded with and ended up disappointing a lot of people after making promises. The charm Dike Iwuala laid against him got a strong hold of him.

Weeks later, before sunrise in the evil forest of Achi, a pregnant lioness was going through labour pains and needed a place to settle before giving birth. She searched but found nowhere suitable to stay, she carelessly forced herself underneath the big 'Oji' tree and rested on the spot where Dike buried the charm. Like a turned-off electric switch, the power behind the charm vanished and chief Uzonna instantly regained his senses while sleeping in his house.

Though he did not remember much, but he knew that that day was a market day because he had a market day calendar. He quickly got himself ready and followed his humble servants to the market for business. While in the market place, chief Uzonna's mind was not at ease because he felt that something had gone wrong. So much that it had affected his business.

As answer was what he needed or else, he would be left in a dilemma. These worries made him leave the market place before the closing hours at sunset. He began to walk aimlessly in confusion as if the charm was still working on him. He passed by the village stream and was carried away by the sight of a beautiful girl that he saw, she was the type that filled his dreams for many night-tall, fair in complexion and beautiful as a river goddess. She was wearing a wrapper which covered her from breast to knee with a girdle around her waist, leaving the rest of her beautiful skin exposed.

Around her neck and wrist, she wore beaded necklace and bangles and on her neatly plaited hair was a ribbon made of string and flower petals. She was referred to as the 'figure that set even an impotent's loin on fire.'

Chief Uzonna was so carried away by the girl's stunning beauty that he had to approach her, "Nne, please come," he called her politely. The girl walked to the chief and bent on her knees as a sign of respect.

"What is your name?" the chief asked.

"Nwakaego" she replied innocently.

"Nwakaego, actually I was charmed by your beauty, let me ask you, how would you like to be a chief's wife?" chief Uzonna asked her plainly.

Nwakego in her early twenties had expected a suitor to approach her soon but to her least expectation it happened to be a chief who took her by surprise.

She felt embarrassed by the chief's proposa as she blushed but seemed to like it too.

"Nze, I .....er.... I don't know what to say," she spoke shyly.

"I'll tell you what; tell your parent, especially your father that I'll come over to his place immediately the sun sets."

"My parents are no more" Nwakaego replied sadly. "I was left in the care of my uncle, Dede Ndudi."

"I am sorry to hear that," chief Uzonna consoled.

"Thank you," Nwakaego replied

"I think I know your uncle," chief Uzonna noted the name sounded familiar. Tell him that I would be coming to see him by sunset, okay?"

"Yes, Nze," said Nwakaego before leaving.

Nwakaego felt very happy as she went. Immediately she arrived, the first thing she did was to tell her fellow spinster- friends about the fortunate thing that happened to her. She also told her uncle as soon as he returned from the market that evening. Her uncle's answer was positive and both of them joyfully awaited chief Uzonna's arrival.

That evening, chief Uzonna visited Nwakaego's Uncle, they talked over the issue at length and drank the local palmwine that the chief presented as his proposal token. The marriage preparations soon started after chief Uzonna
informed the head chief and other chiefs of his coming wedlock.

Soon, the marriage date was fixed and many people who had been eager to witness the day that chief Uzonna would get married turned out in their numbers for the occasion. Both well-wishers and enemies alike were around. Dike had come too and as usual, he was watching from a distance.

As chief Uzonna stepped into Ndudi's compound the crowd that had gathered there hailed and cheered him, so did the other chiefs who accompanied him.

They waved back at the crowed and made their way to the special seats reserved for them.

Meanwhile, Nwakaego was inside her stepmother's hut with her friends and most of the elderly women who were getting her ready to be presented to her husband-to-be.

The headchief was also around to see that the marriage ceremony was performed according to their tradition. This was because the marriage involved a chief and other chiefs were around to witness the occasion. The bride-price was settled in the traditional way, accompanied by a few goats that were given to the major groups in the village that were present, such as age-grade groups from the bride's side and titled men from all over the region.

Towards the end of it all, Nwakaego was ushered in with a cup of palmwine to identify her chosen one and give him the cup to drink from and return the rest to her to finish. While she went about the task, others in chief Uzonna's entourage jokingly tried

to lure her to give them the cup of wine. She refused and only let go of the cup when she had knelt down in front of her suitor, chief Uzonna. After she had done this, everybody hailed her. Then came the time to find out if she had retained her maidenhood. Many young girls were left unmarried after failing the test of maidenhood; this was because they had affairs before wedlock. It was only on rare cases that a few of them still got married probably because of their beauty, good character or in most cases the ability to work hard. But it was prestigious for man to marry a virgin. Nwakaego was asked to go round a mounted staff seven consecutive times and at the same time swear that she had not had any amorous relationship with any man. She was also successful in that test and the whole gathering cheered and hailed her again, including her proud uncle. At the end of the important traditional ceremony, chief Uzonna paid eight shillings as the bride-price that had been decided earlier with his in-law. The headchief then got to his feet to make a speech, "I greet you all, people of Aboh. As you all know, today is when we join the hands of our son and daughter in matrimony, and we also know that it is not easy for young people who are just married to enjoy marital bliss without the wise guidance of we the elders. The time has come for us to advise them on what getting together means." The headchief called the bride and groom and spoke to them "Ego, my daughter you've made your mind that you're going to stay with Uzonna for the rest of your life, haven't you? Nwakaego nodded shyly

"Will you honour him, love and be faithful to him

till you die?" "Yes," she answered again. The headchief prayed for them. As they knelt down, he called on the gods of the land to bless and guide them throughout their days together. After the prayer, the couple went back to their seat and the 'OKROSHA' cultural dance entertainers took the stage. They ran into the compound and positioned themselves for the commencement of their dance presentation. They stood still like statues; remaining motionless until their leader snapped her finger, giving them the right signal to begin their performance. The colourful dancers started to dance vigorously and they thrilled the audience all day long.

CHAPTER FIVE

The Unknown Births
of the Shrine Babies

Months after the marriage ceremony of chief Uzonna and Nwakaego, she conceived. The awaited baby special. This was because, chief Uzonna, due to his popularity was a special person in Aboh and so was Nwakaego, due to her stunning beauty.

So the coming together of the two special people as husband and wife convinced everyone that the couple's child would be one in a million. All eyes waited and watched anxiously to witness the arrival of the lucky baby.

It was the 88th anniversary of the laying of the 'IKECHIALA' (power to rule a land) shrine, in the council hall of Aboh, it was also a market day but the people had decided to declare that day a market —free day due to the anniversary of the Ikechiala shrine. But in the very early hours of that day, Nwakaego's screams were heard by her husband. Chief Uzonna rushed with a matchet to her hut, thinking that intruders were attacking his beloved wife. However, he arrived to meet Nwakaego alone, moaning in pains.

"Oh! It.......it's coming out......Nze...... where are you?" she was twisting herself on the floor in agony and was perspiring all over her face, she was in labour.

"The baby? ....no! Today is the sacred anniversary of the Ikechiala shrine, hold on Ego until tomorrow, please, don't let the baby come out or it will be killed," chief Uzonna pleaded. He was afraid that the baby would be killed because no baby born on any sacred anniversary of the Ikechiala shrine was spared. This was because only those born on the sacred days of the shrine's anniversary could destroy it, so the villagers feared the mistake of having the shrine destroyed and killed any child born on those days.

Nwakaego could not stop the baby from coming out because she was dying in pain and screaming.

Chief Uzonna paced about the room, confused. He did not know whether to go out and call for help, or to remain and pet his laboring wife because he feared a helper could reveal the secret which could cost him his baby's life. As he remained without knowing what to do, his wife moaned as if she was stabbed and immediately the baby's head appeared. Uzonna wasted no time as he soon realized that he was supposed to help his wife with the delivery. He did all he could even though he was inexperienced in helping with the delivery until the baby came out safe and sound.

He cleaned up the baby, who was a baby boy, and laid him by his mother who was resting from the terrible experienced she just had. Exactly an hour later, while chief Uzonna was trying to put things in order, his wife began to scream in pain again. It was

another labour and another child was arriving. Chief Uzonna stood and aided her with the birth of the second baby who was also a boy. He cleaned him up as well and laid him next to the first one. Though, chief Uzonna's wife gave birth to handsome babies, he was not quite happy because they were born on a forbidden day. He knew their lives were in danger if the news about their birth is exposed to the public. He decided to hide the twins for two days after which he would tell the villagers about their birth, which will be two days later than the anniversary of the Ikechiala shrine. His plan worked and the people believed him and even congratulated him. No one had doubt or suspected because they believed that Uzonna's ways were transparent.

Chapter Six

A New Head Chief is Made

Now three years passed after the birth of the twins, Arinze and Nwanze were their names. Many strange signs showed in the village of Aboh to reveal their birth day. Such as an owl that appeared in the day at   the council hall, a hen that feared no one in the village except Arinze and Nwanze and the seldom falling of rain and the sun shining simultaneously.

A lot of other strange and unusual things happened but the villagers of Aboh failed to comprehend why. No one's thought came to the birth of chief Uzonna's babies, not even the Mmbe (tortoise) Dike Iwuala. He had always been looking for a way to destroy Uzonna and if only he knew about the birth of the babies, he would have happily told everyone. The children were growing rapidly and bore striking resemblance to their father, chief Uzonna.

Chief Uzonna loved his two handsome sons but feared that the truth about their birth could be unveiled someday. Even if the villagers did not know, the gods knew.

Nwakaego was busy preparing the evening meal while chief Uzonna watched the kids as they played.

They heard the town crier's voice; "people of Aboh, the headchief has called for an emergency

meeting of the chiefs now. As usual, no one is expected to be seen around the council hall," he beat his gong and proceeded. Because the meeting was said to be urgent Uzonna quikly got ready and went for it.

He met the other chiefs seated and waiting for the arrival of the headchief. When the headchief came he looked pale, depressed and sick, he did not dress in his usual chieftancy outfit. All he wore was wrapping cloth which he tied on his skinny body and knotted the two ends on his left shoulder. He also tied a girdle around his waist. The headchief coughed slightly while trying to clear his throat and began to speak.

"Greetings, my honorable chiefs, I know you'll be eager to know why I have summoned this urgent meeting. All of you are not here as I can see, probably because the information about the urgent meeting has not reached

the ears of others. However, we must go on."   The headchief walked slowly to his throne and sat in it, then continued. "I called you to tell you that my time to join our ancestors is at hand. I regret it but i must obey the call. The practices of this cult must continue, lest the gods become angry. Nothing should deter you from doing this. The gods have permitted me to appoint a new leader who will succeed me. He is in the person of Chief Uzonna Udo and that is because he has the higher number of maize grains remaining on his cobs which means that his time of stay before joining our ancestors is longer than that of the rest of you." The headchief stood up again and walked slowly behind his throne before breaking a
shocking news.

"But before that is fulfilled the gods request a sacrificial rite which has to do with his sons."

"No!" shouted chief Uzonna defiantly, "I have sacrificed my life for the cult and may not live after seven years from now, and you still want me to give my sons as sacrifice" the other chief turned and looked at him, they were surprise at his outburst.

"Nzeukwu, please, plead with the gods on my behalf to pleas spare my sons. Ever since I became chief I have not really been myself, or is it wrong to be a chief?" Uzonna begged. He knew that the birth day of his two sons were improper and against the laws of the land, which was why the gods wanted their lives. But none of the other chiefs knew that.

Chief Uzonna impatiently said you can let somebody else be the new headchief. I am not interested if it will cost me my sons lives," and he angrily walked away.

He was lucky that he walked out of a casual meeting. Were it to be during the cult general meeting, the gods would have struck him dead instantly.

When Uzonna got home that night, he could not sleep, he was so worried that he laid still, thinking deeply. His wife came into his hut and noticed his countenance. Uzonna told his wife about the chiefs' cult. He was the first chief in history to walk out of a meeting and he warned her not to tell anybody. He also told her about how his own life would come to an end in the next seven years and what they had told him to do with his sons before they would formerly

recognize him as the new headchief.

"Isn't there way of stopping your death at that appointed time?" Nwakaego asked fearfully.

There's no way of stopping this because I've given my soul to the gods, I've also observed that that there is something else wrong with me which you don't understand. Sometimes I feel that everyone around me is foolish and I notice I keep misbehaving at such times. The next moment I'll be back to my senses. I don't know what is wrong with me"

The process of his constant change of attitude was caused by the lioness that settled on the spot were Dike buried the charm in the Achi forest. Whenever the lioness moves from the spot to search for food for her off springs, the charm will begin to manifest causing the negative attitude of chief Uzonna to emerge, but as soon as the lion settles back on the spot, Uzonna gains back his senses. The lioness stay was an obstruction to the effect of Dike's charm.

Uzonna watched his wife shedding tears for him, the sadness was the event of the night. Finally, he told his wife to take his children far away from him whenever she became aware of such strange manifestation because he knew that he would surely take them to the gods in that state. Nwakaego sorrowfully spent the night by her husband's bedside while the kids slept in her hut.

Hours later, the lioness and her cubs left the spot where the charm was buried. At the same moment in chief Uzonna's house, he got up and looked around and saw his wife sleeping beside him.

"How did this woman get here? Doesn't she have a sleeping place" he asked angrily.

I think she must be out of her senses to come into my hut. I, the ISHI AGU I of Aboh land" he screamed and roughly woke her up.

"What do you want?" he asked her harshly.

"Your highness, what is wrong?" she asked in a sleepy tone.

"I said you should explain why you have slept in my hut," chief Uzonna barked sharply, Nwakaego finally became wide awake.

She quickly remembered what Uzonna had told her earlier that night and ran to the twin kids, she ran with them to her friend's place for safety.

Nkechi was the woman she took them to and after explaining the reasons, she went back in search of how to deal with Uzonna's mental ailment.

Two days later, a sad news reached chief Uzonna that the headchief was dead, chief Uzonna quickly went to the council hall where he met the other chiefs sitting sorrowfully with the corpse of the headchief lying in front of them. He sat down quietly and maintained the usual position. A few minutes later, chief Obidike got up and spoke;

"Fellow chiefs of Aboh clan as you can see, a sad thing has befallen us. We should be calm and not let the fear of it disturb us, even if we all know what has happened. It will likely happen to each an every one of us when it's our time. Tonight, as it is our tradition, we should all take his body to where it will be buried and do the burying and funeral ceremony. Then we shall all return and crown chief Uzonna, the new headchief

as proposed by the gods," at that they all dispersed.

Very late that night they all went to the graveyard of the headchief and had him buried, accompanied by the usual burial rites. The next morning, all the chiefs gathered and Uzonna was made the new headchief. He moved to the palace with his wife but did not remember that he had children. Adding to the fact that he was supposed to become richer since he was now the new headchief, but he did not know that because he was still under the influence of the charm. He simply remained rich on the average and also suffered sever loss of memory. Nwakaego was always busy thinking hard and trying to find a way of restoring her husband's senses to normal. Wherever she went, the answer was that there was nothing that could be done. She remembered the evil herbalist that lived near the forest of Achi though it was said that the man preferred performing harmful charms to curing people. She decided to give him a try. That herbalist was as deadly as Ezearu (king of evil) because he was Ezearu himself, the one known as Ezenmo (king of spirit). Nwakaego went to him for help, but woe, he was the last kind to be of good help to a human being.

Chapter Seven

Insanity Befalls Dike

Nwakaego's kids remained under the custody of Nkechi, her friend. For once, the kids had thought the stay was for few days, but as weeks rolled by, they began to dislike the idea of being away from their real home, a place that was more comfortable with their biological parents. They were just three year old kids and hadn't enough boldness to tell Nkechi how they felt about staying with her. They only complained to their mother each time she visited. Nwakaego too did not like it as her kids were far from her, but the gods were desperately persuading the headchief , chief Uzonna, to make a sacrifice of his children.

Uzonna, for what had been disturbing him, did not remember that he had kids. The charm had so badly affected his brain that he saw his wife Nwakaego as a maid and not a wife, if not; there was every tendency that they would have had more children,

*   *   *   *

*   *   *   *

Now, five years passed with all the troubles that Nwakaego was encountering, her husband had suffered a lot from the gods' wrath due to the fact that he did not bring his children for sacrificial purposes. Even his looks revealed his suffering and a fast

ageing body that he got in the process, growing very slim like one suffering from a dreadful disease and weak like a seventy-eight year- old. The villagers were surprised at what was happening to the young looking headchief they used to have. None knew except the chiefs themselves who could do nothing because Uzonna was the headchief and had access to the rocky shrine. His punishment was from the gods and the certainty of his death was to come very soon. Nwakaego was always so bothered that she kept on crying everyday, not only for the anticipated death of her husband, but for how she would suffer alone with her kids who were born on the anniversary day of the Ikechiala shrine. She was scared of others finding out because they would certainly have the rites performed with the kids, and if followed by her husband's certain death soon, she would be left with nothing and no one.

Arinze, the first of Nwakaego's twin kids grew to be a stubborn eight-year-old kid, he didn't like the idea of being sent around to do domestic work in Nkechi's house. He was wiser than an average child of his age and knowing that his mother cherished them so much, coupled with the fact that he was the son of the headchief, he saw it degrading going on errands. In contrast to Arinze, his twin brother, Nwanze was gentle and went on every errand that he was sent. As a result of that, Nkechi always made sure that Nwanze's food was more than Arinze's. Arinze did not care because he could fend for himself at eight years, even though Nkechi restricted his movement.

Arinze decided to find out what was wrong with his family as he began to indulge in he idea of running away from Nkechi to his long-left home. He told Nwanze, his twin brother about the plan but Nwanze tried to talk him out of it. He could not stop Arinze because Arinze was a hard nut to crack, instead Arinze succeeded in convincing him and told him that no one was going to spot them, or take them to the shrine because they knew why they were not being allowed to go out.

The following day was 'EKE', another market day and Nkechi had left for the market leaving the boys with her fourteen year old daughter, Ubgomma at home.

As out of sight was out of mind, Ugbomma did not know when the boys left the compound and ran into the bush, seeking freedom. They walked for several hours with the hope of finding another way to their home, but they did not know that they were going astray. They were lost. They roamed about in the bush until Nwanze started complaining of hunger. This made Arinze angry, he did not want to listen to Nwanze as he kept on walking, suddenly he did not here Nwanze's voice again. Arinze turned around and found Nwanze lying on the ground feeling very weak. Arinze quickly ran to him and lifted him up.

"Please don't die, I did not mean to ignore you, get up and let's see if we can find a fruit tree," he begged his brother. Nwanze got up with the help of his brother and together they walked   until they got to a farm where there was an orange tree. Nwanze laid down under the tree while Arinze climbed to get the

fruits, he was plucking the second orange when a passer-by saw them and stopped. The stranger was Dike Iwuala, alias mmbe. Initially, he expected the boys to mock him as every other kids did in Aboh, but because they did not he became curios to learn more about them. After a careful look at their faces he knew that they were Uzonna's children because they resembled their father chief Uzonna. He was really a clever tortoise for figuring that out, unlike every other villager who knew that Uzonna had twin sons. Dike threatened Arinze and ordered him to get down from the tree, pretending that it was his. When Arinze got down, Dike held both of them strongly, each with one hand and took them to his shabby hut. He tied them up and left them on the floor of his hut. They remained in that position untill night time when Dike went to bed. His plan was to take them to the great wizard, Ezearu, the next morning for any possible evil deed. The boys who were awake as a result of freight began to feel the rats in Dike's house crawling on their bodies

"Eeeyy.....they want to bite us," Squealed Nwanze.

"Shut up they are only interested in the ropes, we could be set free when the ropes wear out" figured Arinze.

The rope had a tempting fish- oil smell which attracted the rats. Dike had stolen them for any of his tortoise-like and worthless ventures. Just as Arinze had anticipated, the rats kept eating through the ropes until they got worn out at a point, setting him and Nwanze free from the clutch. As they made to slip

out through the door the noise awakened Dike and he gave them a desperate chase. Dike, though quite sluggishly, caught up with them due to the great age difference and wasting no time that night, he took them to Ezearu.

Ezearu was very pleased when Dike brought the kids to him, he knew how and was willing to waste their lives for especially his own pleasure. But first he would have to consult his living spirits, the existing unseen. Ezearu was displeased after consulting the spirits because he was told to let go of the kids and rather use Dike for the rituals. This was because the twin boys had strong backing as to the fact that their birth was on the Ikechiala shrine anniversary, this means that they could only be used for sacrificial purpose by the gods alone, and Dike, for making the mistake and having the intention of doing away with such kids must face the penalty, failure to do so, the replacement would be Ezearu's head.

Ezearu revealed the grand decision by the spirit, but did not know that he was making a mistake because Dike fled after knowing the implications. Ezenmo had been given until sunrise to perform the rites or die after then. He became stranded and did not know what to do because his spiritual powers had been suspended until after the sacrifice was made. He soon sought to go in search of Dike but it turned out fruitless. Finally, Ezemmo decided to take the kids to the forest of achi, where the charm had been buried and showed them the place. He did not dig it up but told the boys to do so or find someone to do it for them as soon as he lived no more.

Dike ran to mountain caves of the highlands of Aboh. He did it to beat Ezearu's knowledge of where to find him. His intention was to stay there until he had heard of Ezearu' death. But unknown to Dike, just before Ezearu's death, Arinze ran to Achi forest and dug up the charm, he, Dike had buried against his father, Uzonna. The digging up of the charm backfired on Dike in the mountain caves and instantly, he became insane. He tore his clothes, pulled off some of his hair and began to throw himself on the ground.

By then, Ezearu could not move himself again, his bones had become weak and his whole body stiff and lean as if he was suffering from starvation. He told Arinze and his brother to leave and they did so, then they began to trace their way back to the village with the cleverness of Arinze.

A few hours after sunset, Ezearu died. His whole hut darkened and crumbled, forming a large heap of sand over his corpse. At about that time, headchief Uzonna was back to his senses, but only too late because his time of death had come and the gods would come to take him any moment. Meanwhile the news had reached both him and Nwakaego that their kids were missing. Nwakaego quickly ran to Nkechi's house to confirm it. On reaching there, she met Ugbomma, Nkechi's daughter and she told her how it happened, Nwakaego cursed her in anger and blamed her and her mother. But just then, Nkechi appeared with the two boys. She explained how she found them roaming about in the village trying to find their home.

Ego apologized for the anger and insult that she had exhibited and went away with the children to her husband who was almost giving up the ghost as at the

time she left him. Before they reached home, headchief Uzonna, Ego's husband was already dead. The gods had taken him.

Chapter Eight

The New Person

Uzonna's death was a big shock to the villagers of Aboh. The real cause of his demise was known only by the chiefs and his wife, Nwakaego. His ailment was just a means of torture to him by the gods for refusing to maintain the laws of the land until his death. Nwakaego, knowing that the gods were after her kids, decided to take them afar, to Ahbai, a hamlet which had more women than men and their source of living was the rearing of different species of livestock. Nwakaego was allowed to stay there due to her dead husband's popularity, even though they had never seen him before and of course as a widow who was left with the responsibility of taking care of eight-year-old kids. She had to do all she could for them because the children were all that she had left.

*   *   *   *   *   *   *   *   *   *   *   *

Then twelve years after Uzonna's, death many things happened. The village of Aboh only remained lesser than their normal population as there was famine which caused starvation and death. This was as a result of land dispute between them and Ituru, a village close to the gigantic shores of a local river. The Ituru people worshiped the gods of the river. The two villages, Aboh and Ituru, were

quarrelling over some hectares of land in between them. Ituru called for help from their gods, the gods of the river and their prayers were answered by huge rain that fell in Aboh. The rain caused a great flood which wiped a great number of Aboh people, their houses, farms and even two of their chiefs. They were so stubborn that they disagreed with the settlement terms by Ituru which led to their wrath. The gods of Aboh did not render any help to Aboh people. They, the gods were still angry with them because of Uzonna's kids.

Dike Iwuala, alias mmbe, was still insane residing in the mountain caves. As part of his means of survival when insanity took hold of him, he was busy chasing a cave rat until he caught it; "yes, I have you caught you now, what I'll do to you is to take away your precious little life, cook you up and then I'll have a sumptuous lunch," he said vigorously but after reaching his cave-home with the rat, a very deep voice thundered at him;

"Dikeee………the tortoise that chases a rat,"

"Who is calling me?" he asked surprisingly

"it is I, Ezearu, the one known as Ezemmo," and Dike took to his heels, thinking that Ezearu had come for him. He ran as fast as he could until he got tired, but still discovered that Ezearu's voice was still echoing to him.

"What do you want from me? I've nothing to give to you" Dike said as he tried to regain his breath.

"I've come to relieve you of your madness, a decision made by my six spiritual fathers. They have

decided to release you for you have paid enough. I'm ordering you to return to your village and trouble no one again……..do as you're told." And the voice faded away. Immediately, Dike came back to his senses. He looked at himself and saw a man with tattered clothes, bushy and tangled hair and beard, and holding a dead rat. He could even perceive himself smelling terribly. He let go of the rat and turning back, decided to attempt tracing his way back to the village of Aboh. It took him sometime to get to the village because he had almost forgotten the way after spending so much time in the caves. He still managed to find his way to the village and walked into it like a regal king.

The villagers of Aboh knew him and all those he passed by could not help looking at him for more than once because they thought that he had died of his insanity.

He did not talk to anyone even as some of those who knew him trailed him. He went to the place that used to be his hut but discovered that the flood had washed away the left over of his all-around cracked hut. He seemed to remember all the places in the village as he kept on going from one place to another, trying to find a pleasant resting place. By then, those who had nothing doing had formed an entourage-like procession behind him, thinking that he was still mad. An instant thought came to him and he decided to walk to the council hall and see the headchief. That brought about some curiosity in the mind of those that followed him and they did not cease to follow him.

The guards did not allow him to enter because of how strange he was looking, but he began to shout at them, telling them to give him the chance to see the headchief, hence he was a citizen of Aboh.

The dispute soon captured the attention of the headchief who came out to know what was going on.

Dike forced his hands away from the clutch of the guards that held him. On seeing the headchief, Dike knelt down and said, "headchief of Aboh, I seek your permission to stay here in Aboh where I belong, with out troubles." The crowd murmured, wondering how possible it would be for the present headchief to have him stay with them. Aboh villagers loved him to stay because of the fun they made of him, but with the headchief, they could not predict what he would do. Surprisingly, the headchief forgave Dike and in order to keep a close eye on him, he was made a guard in the council hall (palace). The job suited him because it was what he could manage to do than working in a farm which he could not. His laziness contributed to why he was mocked and condemned by his people.

Chapter Nine

The Unlawful Marriage

On Dike's duty post as a guard, few days later, an old man arrogantly approached him,

"You………what are you doing in this village? I thought you're sup-posed to be mad after what you did to my friend Uzonna. Mmbe, answer me, have you left your shell, the caves to come and cause troubles in this village again? If it's your plan, I won't let that happen this time. Amadioha (god of thunder) will surely tear you to pieces,"

Dike was not ready to accommodate any insults so he gave the man a piece of his mind.

"Look here, old man, mind the way you use such insulting words at me or I'll charge you to the headchief for Mmbe is not the old one you used to insult."

"Shame on you if you don't," the man yelled annoyingly. Dike was tempted to strike the man, but he did not, he only left to report to his superior, the chiefguard.

The chief guard came but could not settle the argument. He quickly referred the case to the headchief. The old man was warned never to disturb Dike's peace or face a punishment if he tried it again, so he left looking dissatisfied.

More days elapsed with Dike sticking to his duty post. A little young girl was sent to him to tell him that a woman wanted to see him some short distance from the council hall. But this was a set up. Immediately he got to the place, eight strong men attacked him. He was beaten mercilessly, punched in the eyes and belly, trample on the feet and his head slammed on a hard palm tree. The eight men fled, with the little girl. Dike was left on the floor, bleeding and almost dead. He could hardly move because the beating was more than he could take. He tried to scream for help but no one could come to his aid, even the few people that saw his condition deserted him. It was only when the news got to the palace that the chiefguard rushed and helped with a quick treatment. After that the incident was reported to the headchief who instantly ordered an investigation into the matter by the top spiritualist of the village. The discovery was made and it happened to be pa Ikemefuna who was behind it all, the old man who had threatened Dike previously. He was quickly sent for by the headchief, together with the eight men who did the beating to face the panel of chiefs; all evidences found pa Ikemefuna guilty and because he was an old man he was only asked to pay a compensation of fee of six shillings for himself and four shillings for each of the eight men, all to Dike, the mmbe. Failure to do so that would attract thorough beating in front of all the chiefs and other elders of the land. Pa Ikemefuna paid the money to Dike and was a little bit satisfied because he had dealt with him the way he wanted, though he still wished Dike evil.

Even if Dike had changed, pa Ikemefuna did not care. He still had deadly snares waiting for Dike to step into.

*   *   *   *   *
*   *   *   *

Dike Iwuala saw Nneka going to her friend's place. She was a pretty young girl of nineteen, dark and of average height, but stubborn. She only remembered who Dike was just when he returned recently, but she couldn't picture or remember anything about him even as she had been told about him. Dike was so aroused by Nneka's looks that he decided to make an approach.

"Excuse me young lady," said Dike, and the arrogantly walking Nneka turned round

"Good day," she greeted quite indifferently

"Thank you, I've been noticing you for some time and I think it would be better to know you more closely now" Dike said impressively, " please if you don't mind, I would love to   know your name?"

Nneka was very surprised because she never knew that Dike could be as nice as that, compared to what she had been told about him. Her mind was forced to change due to the gentle and polite impression created by Dike.

The looks on Dike's face revealed that he was much interested in her. Nneka knew that she was ripe enough to be married to a man very soon and it happened that the man standing in front of her looked very much interested; all she needed to do was to give him the chance.

"My name is Nneka," she spoke, tracing the ground with her foot.

"What a lovely name, mine is Dike,"

"Dike Iwuala, alias mmbe," she added.

"That's true, you seem to know me well like almost all other villagers"

"I know you but not very much." Nneka delightfully said. She was beginning to show some excitement in the little relationship between the two of them.

Dike was ready to start proposing to her, but he needed to be sure she was not engaged to any man

"Are you married? He asked.

"No, you are the first person that's asking me this question," she confessed. Dike instantly proposed to her and because she expected it and was pleased with his manners, she accepted the proposal with a smile. Though she didn't have the final say because that right belonged to her parents. Deep down in her mind she was willing to be Dike's wife at that instance, so the first step to take was to seek her father's consent and that was Dike's duty.   Nneka got home and told her father that a man was interested in marring her. Her father was delighted and asked Nneka to bring him so that he and his family could see the man. Two days after their first meeting, Nneka took Dike to see her parents.

Dike looked very happy as he dressed in his best attire which was a brown flowered wrapper he tied round his waist. He carried along a keg of palm wine to show respect and loyalty to Nneka's parents, as it was part of the tradition and also to win their heart and acceptance as a prospective son-in-law. Dike sat on a mat in the compound and kept thinking of how he would make his initial formal visit a success while Nneka went to call her father. She returned with her father and unexpectedly, Nneka's father shouted at Dike.

"You again! What are you doing in my house?' Dike now frightened couldn't give an answer to that question as he saw a fierce and aggressive look on Nneka's father. Nneka's father, pa Ikemefuna, quickly went into his hut to fetch his machet, but before he could do that, Dike had fled. He gave Dike a little chase but couldn't catch him because he was aged and almost weary.

He however went back to warn his daughter against Dike. "Nneka, why do you want to marry that evil man?" he yelled. "Don't you know he killed my best friend, the only man my old age depended on? I've made him my sworn enemy"

"I never knew that you hated him!" Nneka yelled back, "but father, he is harmless he's a good person and I would want to have him as my husband" Nneka said this time with a softer tone

"If you ever repeat that, I will break your head with this matchet," pa Ikemefuna warned furiously. Nneka didn't want to listen and agree with him. She didn't want to believe anyone who said Dike was bad because Dike had been nice to her. She had been blindfolded by his love for her. Her father's rejection of Dike could erupt her uncontrollable stubbornness to the extreme, after keeping cool for the past few weeks. Without hesitation therefore she ran away from the house.

Dike, on reaching home, locked himself in is hut and thanked his creator for saving him from the

dangerous hands of pa Ikemefuna. He swore never to have anything to do with   Nneka again.

Meanwhile, Nneka had run to the palace where Dike was working as a day-guard but was disappointed to notice he was absent, and to make matters worse, she didn't even know his house, otherwise she would have gone there to look for him. Out of grief and heart ache, she slowly walked to a nearby tree and sat underneath it. Nothing else ran through her mind except thoughts of Dike, feeling sad and lonely, she began to cry as she sang.

"MY FATHER, MY FATHER
WHY DO YOU WANT TO TAKE
MY LOVE AWAY FROM ME?
MY FATHER, MY FATHER
WHY DO YOU WANT TO DENY ME
 MY FUTURE WITH THE ONE I LOVE?
IF THERE'S ANYTHING WRONG HE
DID TO YOU PLEASE FORGIVE   HIM FOR   MY SAKE.
IF YOU ARE REALLY MY FATHER

PLEASE LET ME MARRY HIM"

Meanwhile, pa Ikemefuna was at home, cursing and vowing seriously, "I swear by the gods of the land that this demon called Dike will not marry my daughter. He can't have his way for the second time after what he did. I just pray that he falls one more time into my trap and I'll surely strike him dead." As he continued making endless utterances about Dike, his hands and legs began to shiver like

someone who had caught a high fever. His body temperature began to rise. Suddenly he dropped on the floor and started omitting foam from his mouth. Nneka's immediate younger brother, Abagana, came in to serve the evening meal to his father and discovered his deplorable state. He quickly called his mother who came running and both of them helped pa Ikemefuna off the ground to a more comfortable position. A native doctor was quickly sent for to commence instant treatment on him.

At sunrise, Dike quickly made for the palace where he worked, he had no peace of mind after what happened the previous day. He was still contemplating on whether it was a plan or coincidence.

His thoughts were suddenly interrupted by the unexpected sight of Nneka who was coming from a distance. In order to keep to his word of not wanting to have anything to do with her again, he pretended not to have seen her and turned his face to the opposite direction, frowning. When she got close enough, looking pale, she tried to beg for his forgiveness and to convince him that what happened was not her expectation. "Dike please I'm sorry for what happened yesterday, I never knew that you and my father were not in good terms" she begged. Dike remained mute and had a dense look of hatred in his eyes.

Nneka was not discouraged. She still continued to speak; "Dike, why won't you talk to me? I wasn't the one that offended you, I beg for your mercy, Dike."

Dike's heart was responding to the agonizing plea of Nneka but he didn't want to show it, even as she went on her knees and cried. There was nothing else she thought she could do to convince him, but believed that she had lost her first man, her first love. She stood up with tears gushing down her cheeks and she began to walk away.

She started to sing another song:
"MY FATHER, LOOK AT WHAT
YOU'VE DONE TO ME, THE MAN YOU
HATE IS THE MAN I LOVE

I WANT NO ONE ELSE BUT HIM
YOU DENIED ME MY LOVE, OH
BELOVED FATHER BUT WHO ELSE COULD I LOVE?
OH! FATHER LOOK AT WHAT
YOU'VE DONE TO ME!"

Dike was moved by the wordings of that song. He couldn't hide his feelings any more. He didn't' want her to go away because love had taken hold of him in such a magical hurry that he called her, "Nneka." She turned and Dike walked to her and took her by the hand. Wiping away her tears, he expressed the regret for not listening to her.

At pa Ikemefuna's house, he was still lying down sick with his wife by his side who was very worried about his condition. When he eventually woke up, the first thing he did was to try to instigate his wife to stop Nneka their daughter from getting married   to Dike.

Nneka had made up her mind to stay out of sight, but before that she had already had secret

meetings with Dike and when Dike became aware of the implications, he politely told her to stay away from him for some time, until things became normal.

Pa Ikemefuna's ailment kept worsening daily, even with all the expensive treatment given to him, everything done proved abortive. That demoralized Nneka's mother herself because she was experiencing symptoms of high blood pressure, due to her husband's ill health and her daughter's disappearance. She was also confused as to which problem to start solving with the little amount of money that she had, it was a very heavy burden for a soft hearted woman like her to carry.

After about eight weeks of desertion from home, Nneka returned to the village, but she did not want to go back to her father's house because of her protruding stomach which was as a result of her intimate affair with Dike before she fled. On learning of her returned Nneka's mother was over joyed and quickly sent for Nneka to return home and see her and at least talk to her sick and dying father, with the hope that it could revive him.

Nneka went home after receiving the message. It was very irresponsible of her to have gone home to her parents with a pregnancy belonging to man she had not married. The tradition despised it and it brought shame to any family who had someone that has broken   the tradition.

As Nneka entered the hut where her father was lying, Ekemma, Nneka's mother whispered to her husband's ear that their run-away daughter had returned. The weak and sickly pa Ikemefuna smiled and cast his eyes towards the door's entrance where Nneka stood smiling back at him. The smile on his face grew wider with joy. He was about to speak when his eyes fell on Nneka's protruding stomach, at once, the glowing smile on his face disappeared and without thinking, he jumped out of the wooden bed, against the doctor's warning. He landed badly, crashing his chest on the bare floor. Every where was silent as pa Ikemefuna laid motionless on the ground. Much to a temporal relief for his wife, he slowly lifted   himself and then pointed a trembling hand at Nneka's stomach.

"Nneka, what is this?" he asked in disbelief.

"Father I am pregnant," Nneka replied

"For who?" the old pa Ikemefuna asked

Nneka was foolish for revealing that the pregnancy was for Dike, the dreaded enemy of pa Ikemefuna. To make matters worse she also brought shame and abomination to the family. The old and weak pa Ikemefuna could no longer bear the tragedy his daughter had brought upon him. All he could mutter was "Nneka, after all I told you, Nneka ….…..after all that I told you…"

He jumped to the ground after a short while, he gave up the ghost. Pa Ikemefuna was dead.

Pa Ikemefuna's demise painfully widowed his two wives, Nneka's mother and her mate. As they told sympathizers it was the time for him to die.

The blame was no doubt on the stubborn and disrespectful Nneka. She was so confused that she ran out of home after her mother had angrily cursed her, telling her that she'd   never find happiness in her

life again.

Because of the pregnancy, love and security she believed to have gotten from Dike, she ran back to him. Dike thought at least he could settle with Nneka's mother, but was surprised when she walked him out of her compound on his first visit to see her. Nneka's mother went as far as calling him a wizard and also blamed him for the death of her husband.

Chapter Ten

Quest For Return

Ahbai became a second home to Nwakaego and her two sons .she knew that anytime she returned to Aboh with her children, they would be sacrificed to the gods of Aboh. The last thing she could think of was to return to Aboh. Even after her kids had become grown-ups at nineteen years of age. Though she constantly reminded them of their father land which they knew but going back was something that she strongly advised them not to do.

Arinze grew up to be a strong, muscular and brave man. He always had in his mind that he would go back to Aboh, not to stay but to experience the joy of living in his father land, his birth place. He had every single information about the happenings in Aboh through the inter town traders.

One day, while Arinze was sitting at home after his mother had gone to visit a neighbor, he reflected on the past happenings that led to their flight from Aboh. Arinze was angry about the message he received that Dike was well again and was finally making good use of his life. Another thing that angered him more was when he learnt how Dike had caused pa Ikemefuna's death, infact to Arinze, Dike had done enough and needed to be paid back in his own coin. All Arinze wanted to do was to destroy Dike. If Dike clamed to be bad, he was worse.

Arinze felt it was his duty to avenge his late father's death and hence he began to make out plans to eliminate Dike.

Chapter Eleven

The Hero

One early morning while Dike was at his normal place of work, the palace, he overhead some whispering voices, "No.......we will take the back door, tie up all the servants and guards one at a time, and we'll go into the room and get the things or do you see any problem with that plan?" said one of the voices.

"It's okay by me," agreed another voice.

"Me too," added another.

"It will be perfect, so when are we coming back for the operation?" asked the last of the voices.

"When the chicken must have gone to roost, we would wait for the day to get darker, then we'll strike," concluded the leading voice. The conversation revealed an evil plan. Dike whispered what he heard to no one. He kept it to himself to think of a way of trapping them; it was a good quality that he had, cleverness. That was why he was nicknamed "Mmbe" (tortoise)

When it got dark at about ten p.m. four masked men slid silently over the walls of the palace.

They quietly took their positions and one after the other, they caught and tied up the servants and guards, including the chiefguard himself. They broke into the dark room and felt the Ikechiala shrine as it

stood on its own, erect. Because it was not what they were looking for, they went on their knees and began to feel for the object that contained the magic powers, a piece of python skin which was very magical because it could make any wish come through in an instant.

Dike, who was not among those that were tied up, came out from the place he had hidden and

sneaked into were he knew they would be, the dark room. As he came close to the narrow door of the dark room, he could hear the four men cautiously searching the room. They had left no one to keep a watch in case any of the trapped men got freed by any possible means. Dike pushed the door of the dark room and shut it. He trapped the men in the dark room and freed his fellow guards. All of the palace guards fetched their knives and spears and blocked   the exit of the dark room. The thieves forced the door open after Dike had swung the wooden latch that held them captive. They were surprised to see the whole guards waiting for them.

"Seize them" barked the chiefguard, and they were caught, tied and locked to await the headchief's judgment. The thieves were first tortured so that they would reveal were they came from and what their mission was, but they were stubborn even when their heads were dipped into pots of water for minutes. Soon enough the weakest among all of them could not take the punishment any longer, so he confessed their mission and revealed that they came from Umadai.

Umadai was one of the most hated villages in the eastern part of Nigeria. Their soil was not good for farming and rearing of animals, so that made them poor. Most of their villagers depended on other villages for food. Some of the villagers stole from other villages, but   their pride did not make them acknowledge that many villager were richer than they were. This pride of theirs made other villages hate them.

The headchief of Aboh as a reward freed the thief that confessed and had others kept under custody for something that only the chiefs and the gods knew about.

Before night fall, the headchief sent the village crier to assemble the other chiefs for a late night meeting, so as to perform the occultic rites with the   thieves.

During that period, Dike as a newly appointed second-in-command to the chiefguard, was busy going round the palace to make sure that everything was in place. He came across where the meeting was being held and discovered that all the chiefs had entered into the dark room without their clothes. He wondered what the chiefs would be doing in the mysterious dark room without their clothes. Dike was tempted to betray the chiefs and reveal what was happening in the dark room. Dike Iwuala the mmbe himself could never keep his mind from evil thoughts. He was always concerned with the deed of the darkness. But like every other evil deeds of his, he got evil returns.

Ikenga, the luckiest of the four thieves had run back to his village, Umadai. He made straight for the palace and hastily confessed his sins to the headchief. He also pleaded with their headchief to rescue his other friends from Aboh and punish them rather killing them, which he was sure they would do. The headchief was really bitter about the news so he angrily rejected being of help to Ikenga's friends because that had brought shame to their clan. But

after the headchief consulted his cabinet of chiefs, it was agreed that the meeting should be arranged between the two villages. A date for the meeting was fixed and the headchief of Aboh took his chiefs and some guards to Umadai for the meeting. They went to honour the invitation from Umadai. The chiefguard went along with them and the protection of the palace was under the care of Dike, the second-in-command. This was because he gained their trust.

Dike's long awaited time had come. The time to discover the things in the dark room, he made his way to the dark room without anyone noticing him. With the aid of the small lamp he carried, he saw different kinds of charm and other mysterious object on the floor and walls. He also saw the stone shrine standing majestically in the center of the room. He knew the shrine because he had been hearing about it, but that was his first time of seeing the seven-feet high idol.

In Dike's mind, the first thing that came up was to search for the magic charm, the python skin that made the thieves to come all the way from their village. He took his time and found it because he was not in a hurry. He knew that no one would come around there. With the python skin, he started doing wonders.

At once, he commanded the charm to open to him the activities of the shrine, and like magic, a parrot emerged and revealed to him all that he wanted to know. He then new how to recite the incantations that both opened and closed the shrine, and also the function of many of the charms hanging

on the walls and floor of the dark room. He recited the incantations that opened the shrine, and worked into it, bowed to the gods and asked them to give him more magical powers. All his request were granted to him and after he had taking the oath of making the usual sacrifices. When he finished and came out, Aboh village remained under his firm control.

Chapter Twelve

The War

In Umadai, while the chiefs of Aboh were waiting for the commencement of the meeting, the servants   of the palace of Umadai entertained the guests. The chiefs of Umadai later joined them. The traditional chieftancy salutations were made and a toast was proposed to the Aboh chiefs for honouring the invitation. Soon enough, the issue of the day began and the headchief of Umadai got on his feet;

"Nze ndi Aboh kwenu," he started with the Aboh chiefs.

"Hia!" they collectively answered.

"Nze ndi Aboh kwenu," he said again.

"Hia!" another answer came from them

.."Nnuonu,"

"Hia" they finished.

"I greet and welcome you all," he said delightfully as the Aboh chiefs responded with smiles, nodding their heads majestically. The headchief of Umadai greeted his village chiefs too.

"I've called for this meeting for a reason I assume we all know, but for those who don't know, it is for the release of three of our villagers whom you have held captive. Our people say that if an adult runs and falls down, he is either chasing something or something is chasing him, so these three villagers of ours have fallen down into your traps because they were chasing something in your village. I'm pleading

on their behalf and that of other villagers of our clan for you to release them to us so that we could punish them instead of wasting them in captivity to die. If you want anything in exchange for them, we are ready to give it to you."

The chiefs of Aboh held a small whispering meeting amongst themselves and after that, the headchief of Aboh got up to announce their decision.

"Chiefs of Umadai, I greet you all. We have heard what you said but before I tell you   anything I would like to bring in one of our sayings I learnt from my mother.   She always told me that an ear that refuses to hear goes with the head when it's cut off. There is no village or hamlet that does not know Aboh and her greatness in the eastern region. Your villagers came and trespassed   and like others who did the same, the wrath of our gods have taken hold of them. We are sorry to tell you that it impossible to release them. This is because our gods did not grant us the will to do so, and we will not like to disobey them," he told them plainly and sat down.

The people of Umadai did not know that the men they sought for had already been done away with. They tried in different ways to convince the Aboh chiefs but they did not want to change their decision.

"Even sacrifices of the biggest kind won't change anything," added Ide, who was known as an extrovert among the chiefs in Aboh.

After a long plea by the Umadai chiefs, one of them got angry and said something that sounded like an insult to the gods of Aboh, the headchief of Aboh

felt insulted and decided to end the meeting. He said angrily, "look, chiefs of Umadai, I don't think you are ready to discuss anything with us because if you were you would not be insulting us and our gods. Let us leave this place!" The headchief of Aboh and all his chiefs turned and left the palace, with their host gazing in astonishment. The incident made the headchief of Umadai so angry that he said, "The people of Aboh think they are wise enough. Since they don't want to settle the matter amicably, I think we would have to do it the way they want it. We must get set for war! The people of Aboh can't dominate every village in the eastern region; we have to protect our pride"

Back in the village of Aboh, after Dike had taken over and proclaimed himself as the new headchief, he instantly appointed the new chiefguard of his own, most of the villagers obeyed not only because he was wicked but also because he had the charm of will power, the python skin which he used to over power them . His take-over was swift and well executed. But like every ordinary villager in Aboh, Dike did not know that the chiefs of Aboh council were a continuous living cult.

The headchief and the other chiefs that went to Umadai returned. On Dike's instruction, they were seized and killed without mercy.

Some weeks later, a message was sent to Dike, the new headchief. An official order was given to him to release the three thieves under their village's custody. The leader of Umadai had no idea that another headchief had forcefully taken over in

Aboh. Dike knew about what the Umadai demanded but could not tell what happened or how the thieves disappeared. He received a couple of war threats, especially when he replied telling them he knew nothing about the captured thieves. But when the threat became too much he called a meeting of his cabinet chiefs and declared war on Umadai. Dike felt he had to prove to the neighboring villages that he was not a cowardly leader who would be afraid of village brawls. Dike was pleased to make war. He knew that Umadai was no match to Aboh, especially with a wicked ruler like him in command of the Aboh warriors. Dike saw the opportunity to fight Umudai a as means of proclaiming his emergence and greatness in the Eastern region.

Aboh waited anxiously to invade Umadai and demolish them. They were also careful not to rush into war because they knew that Umadai wanted to take them by surprise, if not, Umudai would have invited them to the battle field of death.

Finally the Umudai drums of war sounded from a distance on the fifth day of the week. Closer and closer, the drum beats increased until the war leader

of the Umadai warriors gave a cat-like war cry. Immediately, the warriors of Umadai rushed into Aboh and started destroying their hut and properties. They were soon surprised to find out that no one came out to defend the destroyed properties and huts. The village was simply deserted as Umadai warriors saw this they gave up their destructive actions to rejoice on having scared off the Aboh natives without losing a single warrior.

Just as they had began to drop their weapons to rejoice more, a sign came and the Aboh warriors came out of their hiding places. They took their enemies by surprise. Before Umadai's warriors could react to Aboh's attacks, many of them had been killed and many injured, some of the remaining ones fled while the rest who were brave enough stood to fight back, but their scanty number could not withstand the whole Aboh army which comprised of a hundred and one warriors. The ones that fought were brave but not strong enough as large stabbings and cuts led to their deaths. The Aboh warriors decided to extend the war to Umudai and there, they killed more and destroyed a lot, burning huts, raiding homes and trampling on farmlands. Soon the war was over and Dike had succeeded in crushing Umudai.

Chapter Thirteen

Evil-Returns

Though most of the Aboh villagers had not been happy because of how Dike killed the former chiefs, peace reigned because they feared to oppose him openly. The people could only gossip about him as the known mmbe, but his presence caused a hell of tension. He went as far as mal-treating his unlawfully married wife, Nneka and had two more wives whom he showed love. This was because the three children that Nneka had for him were all girls, but the new wives had born two male kids each for him.

Sooner than expected, Dike's evil past started hunting him. It was on peaceful night at Aboh, Dike was having a very bad dream and in it he saw Uzonna chasing him with a matchet. No one was willing to help him until Uzonna caught him and cut   off his head. Immediately, he woke up and felt pains all over his body as he suddenly became ill. All he kept hearing was an echo of his name. He could hardly move himself on the wooden bed be-cause of the serious illness. His heart detoriated and that gave him a feeling that something bad was going to happen to him. He moved himself up and went to the shrine to confirm from the gods. He was only told that his past sins were after him and that the disintegration of the great Aboh was at hand. The reason was because

they have failed to fulfill the term of oath to sacrifice Arinze and Nwanze, those born on the shrine's anniversary.

Dike, in staggering weakness came out of the shrine. He sent for his chief guard and ordered him to spread the news all over the village that night, just a few minutes after midnight. When the news got to every Aboh villager, they began to flee from the village one after the other in great fear.

Dike's intention was to assemble his warriors by sunset and have them search for Arinze and Nwanze all over the Eastern region, captured and have them sacrificed to the gods, so that Aboh could still remain united. But beyond Dike's thought and expectation that night, just as confusion riddled the entire village, Arinze suddenly appeared in Aboh, with his army of a hundred and fifty warriors consisting of men and boys. He had set out his long-term plan of eliminating Dike, even if it was going cost him his own life. When Dike saw Arinze, it was as if he was seeing the late Uzonna for the second time because Arinze bore a striking resemblance to his father. Dike's confused warriors were not doing things according to Dike's instructions any longer because a lot of them were busy searching for escape routes with their families before the angry gods of Aboh would send their wrath upon the village. Dike went back to the shrine as fast as his weak body could carry him to ask for powers to destroy Arinze, but he did not know that virtually nothing of the shrine could destroy Arinze because he was born on one of the anniversary days which marked the installation of

the Ikechiala shrine. Arinze had told his men to fight any one who would want to hurt him while he himself would be after Dike. Arinze entered the palace and saw Dike sneaking into the dark room. Arinze cleverly trailed Dike but not too closely. He was surprised when he heard the sound of the shrine opening with no one controlling it. Dike knew very well that Arinze would be behind him so an idea of luring Arinze into the shrine came to his head. It was a good trick conceived by his cunning mind. Fortunately, Arinze had already been informed about the dangerous shrine by his mother, Nwakaego, so he waited to know if Dike would come out and attack him. No noise came from the dark room, Arinze made his advancement into the dark room and saw a deem ray of light coming from the open shrine.

In amazement, he took a peep and saw Dike answering the gods even though Dike looked weak and powerless. Arinze, knowing that he was capable of destroying both Dike and the shrine, ran back, fetched a bush lamb and a spear. He wanted to kill Dike but Dike seemed not wanting to leave the shrine for his own safety and the weakness that had engulfed him. Arinze burnt the Ikechiala shrine together with Dike in it. The flames from the burning shrine caused chaos in Aboh as the shrine crumbled and heated like a burning furnance. In the long- run, the whole natives of Aboh dispersed.

WORD INDEX FROM THE BOOK

Deplorable	Tragedy	Aged
Commence	Mutter	Weary
Previous	Slumped	Furiously
Contemplating	Demise	Blindfolded
Coincidence	Disrespectful	Uncontrollable
Interrupted	Superior	Extreme
Frowning	Recently	Hesitation
Pale	Aroused	Grief
Mute	indifferently	Underneath
Agonizing	Arrogantly	Vowing
Plea	Impressively	Utterances
Gushing	Delightfully	Omitting
Instigate	Excitement	Cunning
Implication	Proposed	Deeds
Ailment	Engaged	Haunted
Abortive	Instantly	Emergence
Demoralized	Consent	Hamlets
Symptoms	Attire	Rumored
Burden	Keg	Intruders
Desertion	Initial	Remote
Protruding	Formal	Depressed
Intimate	Unexpectedly	Yawn
Irresponsible	Fierce	Staggered
Despised	Aggressive	Lamented
Dreaded	Fled	Misfortune
Wearily	Alternative	Ajar
Blankly	Ensure	Hollered
Shrugged	Rituals	Roar
Sighed	Sealed	Loot
Desperate	Dearly	Ganging

Insane	Continuity	Scare
Outskirts	Reshuffled	Slamming
Notorious	Chieftaincy	Retrieving
Herbalist	Crew	Brawls
Blinking	Pledges	Oracle
Stare	Routine	Evidences
Exhausted	Unnoticeable	Increment
Fatigue	Chores	Town-Crier
Injured	Anticipating	Typical
Utter	Extricated	Accent
Appease	Strand	Gong
Gourd	Moulded	
Regain	Prey	Statues
Hospitality	Impatient	Baffled
Morsel	Cope	Gods
Harvesting	Stress	Ancestors
Gossiping	Determine	Traditional
Prosperous	Dispute	Complied
Aiding	Techniques	Shrine
Unseen	Gazelle	Mystical
Knotted	Wander	Incantation
Wiggle	Chirping	Foretold
Repeated	Linen	Taboo
Invisible	Hyena	Shady
Plainly	Collectively	Initiate
Partook	Countenance	Slammed
Forefathers	Offspring	Ghastly
Gruesome	Manifest	Snares
Disperse	Ailment	Cautiously
Unanimously	Clan	Latch
Insinuating	Woe	Extrovert
Comprehend	Biological	Astonished
Attain	Wrath	Amicably
Menacingly	Cherish	Dominate
Suicidal	Degrading	Pompous
Dilemma	Errand	Occurrence
Girdle	Fend	Proclaiming
Loin	Restricted	Destructive
Stunning	Indulged	Maltreating
Suitor	Astray	Haunt
Spinster	Curious	Deteriorated
Usher	Shabby	Disintegration
Entourage	Squealed	Flee

Maidenhood	Clutch	Virtually
Prestigious	Sluggish	Luring
Consecutive	Stiff	Engulf
Amorous	Starvation	Chaos
Matrimony	Crumbled	Immense
Perspiring	Exhibited	Stranded
Paced	Famine	Scores
Seldom	Gigantic	Hefty
Simultaneously	Sumptuous	Forbidden
Unveiled	Vigorously	Elapsed
Summoned	Regal	Intertown
Defiantly	Trailed	Majestically